Larry The Lemon's Lovey And Lowly Little Letters

EILEEN DISTASIO-CLARK

With Great Love and Appreciation to Those Who Have and Do Bless My Life.

My Family:

Joseph DeStasio Sr. & Miriam Lucille Baragone DeStasio, My Late Parents.

Andrea Jean DeStasio McIntosh, My Older Sister and Their Families.

Joseph DeStasio Jr., My Younger and Only Brother and Their Families.

Donna Marie DeStasio Wagner, My Younger Sister and Their Families.

My Children:

Eileen, Rebekah, Rachel, S. Michael,

Jennifer, Sharon, Tara, Stephanie,

Apryll, Mikaelah, & M. Trevor

and THEIR Families!!

ACKNOWLEDGMENTS

First and foremost, I express, deeply, my sincere gratitude to our Heavenly Father for blessing me with the gift and talent of writing! I know I could not do what I do without His assistance.

I also want to acknowledge and express gratitude to my children, Eileen, Rebekah, Rachel, S. Michael, Jennifer, Sharon, Tara, Stephanie, Apryll, Mikaelah, and M. Trevor, who were very active in 'creating' many tales about the Hunk-a-Doodles.

Truth be told, I really do not know how we came up with the name, Hunk-a-Doodles, but I give the credit for that to my children. I must also credit them for the inspirations that produced these stories because it was through their sweet and innocent childhood antics that they were originally originated!

INTRODUCTION

In 1992, shortly after my family moved to Missouri, I found, in a Clearance Sale Bin in the Hy-Vee grocery store, five stuffed fruits: a cherry, a lemon, an orange, a plum, and a watermelon. They were so cute I just had to buy them!

Once home, I put them on the half wall that separated the kitchen from the living room, where they sat for the whole time that we lived in that house. Now, of course, any time we had to move, they did too. We loved them too much to leave them behind!

In different homes, they usually sat in different places, on the wall above the stairs, on a bed, usually mine, on the back of the couch, on... well, just wherever we wanted them to sit. But sitting was not all that they did.

We played with them, we used them to decorate for special occasions, we... well, we just had a great deal of fun with them!

We called them our Hunk-a-Doodles, but I really do not recall how we came up with that name. We also gave each one of them their own name. The cherry was identified as Chad, the orange was named Ollie, the lemon was called Larry, the plum was Peter, and the watermelon was given the name Wally!

We also made up fun stories with them and that is what motivated me to write these stories to share with you! So, please read and enjoy them, over and over and over again!

LARRY THE LEMON'S LOVEY AND LOWLY LITTLE LETTERS

Lovely little Larry the Lemon,
Was quite the Lowly fellow;
Sweet and gentle, kind and caring;
He was quiet, modest, and mellow.

Larry loved to listen to others,
Talk about their life's trials,
Because he always wanted to help them,
Walk all their challenging miles.

So, one of the things that Larry did,
To bring smiles to their faces,
Was writing kind and caring Little Letters,
And leave them, anonymously, at their places.

He cheered them up the best he could,

He helped them with all they needed,

But what brought the warmest feeling to his heart,

Was the joy his letters seeded.

No one knew, not even the other Hunks,

This sweet endeavor by Larry,

So, one day, when his Hunk friends were feeling low,

Letters, for them, he wrote and hid, without any tarry.

'Hey! Wait a minute!!' You are now saying, and I am pretty sure I know why. But I will let you continue so that you can tell me why you want me to wait.

"Well," you are now replying, "we want to know if we can know what Larry put in those letters. So, we are asking you if you can take us to the Hunks home so we can see that."

Yep! That is what I knew you were thinking. And! That is exactly what I was going to do anyway. So, let us be going.

Now, it was not the brightest, most cheery day of all time, but it was also not the gloomiest, most disheartening day either. Yes! There were clouds in the sky, but they were white and billowing. In fact, they looked like pillows. Why, so soft and comfy looking did they appear, that one might think there were angels sitting on those clouds, watching all that was going on at the Hunks' house. And that would have been no surprise to anyone who knew the Hunks because, though they were almost always happy, cheerful, and filled with peace, there were also times when they felt sad, downhearted, and even a little bit lonely.

Now, of course, the day was not really all that gloomy either, a little bit, yes, perhaps, but not really, because, even though there were clouds in the sky, the sun was also shining through and around those clouds, and the sky that could be seen was a beautiful clear blue!!

'So, why then were the Hunks feeling low-down?' You are wondering. Well, this is why.

Even though they all loved having a home, a place where they could be warm when it was cold and cool when it was hot. A place where they could be sheltered when it rained and snowed. A place where Hunks could cook and store their own food, instead of having to hunt for something to eat every day. A place that they could decorate in ways that spoke of them. A place where they could sleep peacefully, and a place that was home, their home, rather than just a wall to sit on day and night, there was something missing.

It had taken them a bit of a while to figure out why they felt... lost... forgotten... alone... Since they were not alone, they had each other, and they were not forgotten, but they felt sad for some reason. They had many friends who came to see them and did things with them. In fact, some of them: like Norash, Eniele, LeChar, ReFinjen, Rata, Lalpry, Rovert, HaKeber, LeAchim, Einahpets, and Haleakim, visited them often! And they were not lost! Either Everyone in all of the Land of Never-Could-Happen and the Valley of Down-Below knew exactly where they lived. But still, somehow, in some way, things were different!

When they had sat on the Lofty White Wall, they were able to see everything that went on in the Land of Never-Could-Happen. They could even watch the happenings in the Valley of Down-Below. They could wave to everyone who passed by, and they could also say Hi! Everyone, as they passed by, waved Hi and said Howdy to them. But, being in their own home, which they truly did love and appreciate, things were different. While they knew they were the ones who should do something to change that, Hunks really did not think they knew what to do. So, that is why they were feeling a little bit downhearted, and that was why they sat—most of the day on most days—on the front porch swing, just going back and forth, and forth and back, and back and fo... well, you know what I mean.

Now, it had not started out that way for them. At first, when they moved into the house, they spent most of their time, almost all day on almost all days, arranging, organizing, decorating, cleaning, cooking, and just enjoying their new home! But after a while, their routine became... well, it just became too routine, and they began to realize that, as important as a home was to them, people were more important. They came to understand why they were beginning to feel... hmmm, what did they feel? They really did not know what it was that they felt. Hunks just knew that whatever it was, they felt it was not what they wanted to feel. Then, after a bit of a while, they realized that what they were feeling was a bit of loneliness, which came as a result of being away from the people in the land and the valley. But what were they to do? What... WERE... they to do? Well, they all thought about that, pondered over it, and prayed about what their options might be.

Then, one morning, when Larry went out to get the mail, as he pulled the mail out of the mailbox, he suddenly had a great idea that they was certain would be the solution. Well, at least one of them, for their struggle. As he walked back to the house, he joyfully cried out, but not too loudly...

"I will write each Hunk a letter, to help them all feel better.

"I will do that right away; I will write them today!"

And that was exactly what Larry did. As soon as he got back to the house, he put the mail on the dining room table and went up to his room, where he spent the rest of the morning writing letters: one to Chad, one to Ollie, one to Peter, one to Wally and the last one to Larry, then he put them in their envelopes and...

'Wait!' You are shouting. 'Why did he write a letter to himself? That seems silly.'

Well, maybe it does seem silly, but it really is not. You see, Larry likes doing good things anonymously and if he wrote the letters that were meant to cheer up the Hunks, but he wrote to only Chad, Ollie, Peter, and Wally and not to himself, they would all know that he was the one who wrote them. Since he did not want that to happen, he wrote a letter to himself too. So, now do you see why?

"Yeah," you are answering. "So, now that we know, please continue to tell us the rest of the story."

Okay, I will be happy to tell you! No! Rather than me just telling you why, we can go back to yesterday, and you can see for yourself what happened.

Are you ready? You are?! Great! Then let us be going!!

By the time Larry finished writing the letters, and Chad, Ollie, Peter, and Wally finished their morning activities, it was time for lunch, which they all had lunch together. Then they spent some time playing a bunch of board games, after which they did their yard work and then, sat down in the Family Room to watch some Old Time Kid's TV shows.

By the time Mr. Hoo-Hoo made a Boo-Boo ended, it was pretty late. So they said their good-nights and headed to their rooms. Once in their rooms, they all dressed for bed, said their personal prayers, got in bed and fell, rather quickly, fast asleep, all, that is, except Larry.

When he was certain that Chad, Ollie, Peter, and Wally were asleep, he picked up all the letters, tip-toed out of his room, up the hall to the stairs, down the steps, through the living room, dining room, and kitchen to the back door, out the door, and across the yard, through the garden, and over the fence to their back-yard neighbor's house. He tapped lightly on their kitchen window and waited patiently for someone to come to the door. Oddly enough, considering how late it was, he really did not have to wait too long before the door opened, and Norash stepped out onto the back porch.

With a bit of surprise and a bigger bit of pleasure in her voice, Norash, upon seeing Larry, said, "Hi, Larry! This is quite a surprise! What are you doing out so late?"

"Hi, Norash!" Larry replied excitedly.

"I have a favor to ask of you.

"I need your help for something I want,

"You and me to do."

"Oh!" Norash said curiously, "What is it you need help with?"

As they both sat down on the back porch step, Larry said:

"Well, maybe you know, or maybe not, but we Hunks
are feeling low.

"So, I came up with a good idea that away the gloom
will blow.

"But I need some help, and I thought of you, 'cause
things you hide so well.

"And I know that you I can trust, my secret not to
tell."

With an increased amount of curiosity in her voice, but also a tone of appreciation, Norash said, "Well, Larry, I am sure you do know that I will never tell anyone anything that I am told to not tell, unless it is something that is wrong and should not be done, and I most certainly would love to help you, because I know that whatever you are doing must be good. You would never do anything that was not good, none of you Hunks would! So, what is it you want me to do?"

After sharing with Norash the details of how all the Hunks were feeling a bit low and explaining to her why they were feeling the way they were feeling. He also told her about the letters he wrote to all of them, including himself. And yes, he also explained to her why he had written a letter to himself. That was when he asked:

"So, Norash, I need to know,

"Will you please hide each letter?

"Then I will have to hunt too,

"And for my plan, that would be better."

"Why, yes!" Norash replied, feeling very honored to be asked to be a part of his wonderfully thoughtful plan. Then, taking the letters from him, she asked, "Is there any place, in particular, you want me to hide them?"

To that, Larry said:

"No, not really; you choose that.

"But please leave for us a clue,

"So that when our search we make,

"Find them, we will be able to do."

Then, after saying their good-nights, Norash went into her house to write the note with a clue on it, so she could hide the letters before she went to bed. And Larry, following his same sneaky, uh, I mean quiet, manner, went back across the yard, into the house, through the kitchen, dining room, and living room, up the stairs, down the hall, into his room, and into bed, where he too fell asleep rather quickly.

Now, when the sun came up to start the day,

The Hunks got up to work and play!

First, they said their morning prayers,

Then they took care of their personal cares.

After that, their breakfast they ate,

Then hurried outside and through the garden gate.

They raked and hoed and pulled the weeds,

And, yes! You guessed it, they found the beads!

'Huh?' You are probably thinking. 'Beads?'

Yes, beads. You see, Norash had come up with a pretty good idea. Rather than just writing a note with a clue on it, she attached strings to the envelopes and on the end of the string was a bead.

She had determined that it would not be a good idea to bury the letters in the dirt; they could get warped from the dew or dirty from the dirt and then not be able to be read. So, she hid the letters in the toolboxes that the Hunks kept along the side of their garden path. Then, she laid the strings out on the ground, each one going in a different direction, and covered them with grass. But they all lead to the same place and that was where she buried the beads.

Got it? You do! Good, now let us get back to the beads!

Well, wait! Before we go back, I think I should tell you that, at this point, Larry was a little bit confused. He wondered where the beads had come from and the strings. He had not given Norash anything except the letters themselves. He was quite confused, just as confused as Chad, Ollie, Peter, and Wally, but for a completely different reason. Ergo, with genuine confusion, he did not know what to expect!

"Hmmmm, what are these?" they all asked together.

As they followed the strings across the nether,

When finally, they came to the boxes of tools,

They opened them up and found more jewels.

(That is more beads.)

*****Side Note:** Norash had also attached a bead to each letter. You see, in order to help the Hunks figure out which letter was his, she thought it was a good idea to match the colors of the beads to their colors. So, the color of the bead on the end of the string was the same as the bead on the letter. There were five colors: red for Chad, orange for Ollie, yellow for Larry, purple for Peter, and green for Wally.

Okay, now that this makes more sense to you, let us go back to the other side and pick up where we left off.

Of course, with the beads, they each found a letter.

And oddly enough, they thought nothing could be better.

'But who,' they wondered, 'would write to us?'

Still, they opened their letters without any fuss.

(And they did know whose letter was whose.)

Once they each had their letter in hand,

They all began to read, and they sounded like a band!

But when they were done, tears were in their eyes,

And each one said, "Oh my goodness, listen to this, guys!"

(Then they took turns reading their letter.)

Now, before reading their letters, they went back to their back porch and sat themselves down on the steps, in the order in which they always sat, or stood, or... well, you know what I mean, and they read their letters, out loud, to each other.

Chad went first, and this is what he read:

Dear Chad, you are as red as a cherry,

And you really do good at making folks merry.

I know you are shy, but you are also sweet too,

I wonder if you would feel better if you do!

What you always have done, go out of your way,

To make others happy and brighten their day.

So, why would you not make joyous days happen,

By visiting people in the Land of Never-Could-Happen?

Yes, you guessed it, this thought is from me!

I sent it to you to make you happy!

Now, stand up real tall and go over the wall,

To visit the friends you have, not one, but all!!

Oh! And of course, I want you to know,

That those in the Valley of Down-Below,

Would love to have a visit from you,

'Cause they love and miss you too!

Your friend,

Me!

Next, Ollie read this letter that was addressed to him:

Dear Ollie, you are as orange as that fruit!

And definitely, its sweetness, you it does suit.

So, perhaps, to yourself, you should give the boot,

And go out with your horn, greetings to toot!

Let the people in the Land of Never-Could-Happen,

Know that you are thinking of them, and not just nappin'.

On their doors, you could also be tappin',

And then leave them a gift in the prettiest wappin'.

I am pretty sure you know who this is,

For, how else could I know your biz?

So, do what you do when you work as a whiz,

22

And with the gift, leave a jar of your fizz!

Oh! And of course, I want you to know,
That those in the Valley of Down-Below,
Would love to have a visit from you,
'Cause they love and miss you too!

Your friend,

Me!

When he was done, Larry read this:

Dear Larry, you are as yellow as a lemon,
But we know you are loved by all the men and
women,
Who live in the Land of Never-Could-Happen,
So, get it together and your wings start flappin'.

Now, by that I know you must know I mean this,
Hustle real fast, so opportunity you do not miss,
To bring joy and pleasure to every Bro and Sis,
Knowing you too will be blessed from their bliss.

So, practice the tunes which will bring the brightest glow,

When sweet music, through your horn, you blow.

And do it for all, not just those you know,

'Cause everyone needs lifting when they are feeling woe.

Oh! And of course, I want you to know,

That those in the Valley of Down-Below,

Would love to have a visit from you,

'Cause they love and miss you too!

Your friend,

Me!

Following him was Peter, and he read:

Dear Peter, you are purple as a plum,

And I know you are feeling a little hum-drum.

But I also know, because around you, I did linger,

That you can change that with your artistic finger.

The people in the Land of Never-Could-Happen,

Love the artwork that you make happen.

So, why do you not sit down and start to draw,

Paintings for your friends, one and all.

And while you are at that, remember this,
Add a message that will bring them bliss.
Good works, I know you do not want to miss,
And this is one, they will all reminisce.

Oh! And of course, I want you to know,
That those in the Valley of Down-Below,
Would love to have a visit from you,
'Cause they love and miss you too!

Your friend,
Me!

Finally, Wally read this:
Dear Wally, a watermelon is striped green like you,
And everyone knows you are that sweet too.
So, this is what I think you should do;
Many good deeds, continuously pursue!

The people in the Land of Never-Could-Happen,

Are probably wondering, 'To you, what happened?'

So, it would be best if, on their doors, you started tappin',

And, when they opened them, just start rappin'.

Talk to them all about everything,

This, that, all the fat, and even nothing.

Then, when you are done with one, another bell go ring,

And hang around to do the same thing.

Oh! And of course, I want you to know,

That those in the Valley of Down-Below,

Would love to have a visit from you,

'Cause they love and miss you too!

Your friend,

Me!

Now, after they were all done reading their letters, they began asking each other who they thought had hidden those letters, but of course, no one really knew. At least it did not seem like any one of them did because they all were suggesting the names of other people who knew them. People from the Land of Never-Could-Happen and the Valley of Down-Below.

But every time one of them suggested a name, another one of them gave a pretty believable reason why that was probably not the right guess.

So, after some time of trying to guess who sent the letters, they all agreed that it did not matter who sent the letters—well, hid the letters. But what was said in the letters is what mattered. So, they all agreed that they were going to begin immediately, that very day, to do all that had been suggested in their letters. They were going to be the ones to reach out to others. They were going to be the ones who would visit, who would help, who would serve, who would give; they would be the ones who would do what they always appreciated being done for them. And that was what they did! From that day on, they were always visiting, serving, helping, giving, and just being wherever they needed to be to uplift others. And it was good that they did, for one day, it all came back to them.

'What?!' You are probably exclaiming. 'Are you saying that the people of the Land of Never-Could-Happen and the Valley of Down-Below did not appreciate all that the Hunk-a-Doodles did for them?'

Well, if that is what you are thinking, think not, because, no, that is not what I am saying. What I am saying is that one day, the tables turned, and this is how that happened.

It was a warm, breezy, early autumn morning and the Hunks were just rising from their wonderful night's sleep. As they always did, they began their day with prayer and personal care. Then they ate their breakfasts and washed their dishes before heading out to the garage to get their rakes so they could 'sweep up' the leaves in the yard and cover their garden bed with them, so the garden could be fertilized throughout the winter. But when they opened the door to the front yard to let in the sun, their joy shone brighter than the sunlight itself.

'Why?' You are probably wondering. Well, this is why.

On their porch were boxes and bags, and knapsacks and cases filled with gifts and treats. There were trays and plates holding food and deserts, and there were cards by the dozens! After a few moments of surprised silence, Chad, Ollie, Larry, Peter, and Wally took the items, all of them, into the house, unwrapped them and read all the cards. Now, since you may be wondering what the cards said, and because not all the cards were worded the exact same way, I will share with you the message that was general to them all, the message that Norash had written and signed, and attached to the gift that she left for them, which, by the way, was a lighthouse, and this is what that was:

Thank you, Chad, Ollie and Larry,
Thank you, Peter and Wally.
You are the greatest friends we have ever had;
When we think of you, we can never be sad.

You have visited us, helped us with chores,
You have given us things that we know were yours.
You have helped us kindly in times of need,
Even cleaning our yard of thorns and weeds.

We are so grateful that you are our friends,
You have taught us so much from beginning to end.
So happy, you make us feel,
Our love for you is ever so real!!

Love to you from all of us in the Land of Never-Could-Happen and the Valley of Down-Below.

Then, just as they finished getting everything inside their house and put it away, there was a knock at the door. They hastened to see who it was and when they opened the door they were stunned. There, standing on the porch, the pathway that led to the porch, and across their front yard were all their friends from the Land of Never-Could-Happen and the Valley of Down-Below, and leading the group was Norash!

Before the Hunks could say anything, Norash spoke up and said, "Okay, Hunks, you cannot say no to our request. We have come to get you because we want you to come with us to Paradise Park, where we have set things up for a great festival. You see, thanks to you and your wonderful example of kindness, we have created a new holiday: Love Others Day, and we want you to be with us for its very first celebration."

Well, needless to say, but I will say it anyway, Chad the Cherry, Ollie the Orange, Larry the Lemon, Peter the Plum, and Wally the Watermelon jumped onto the porch, hopped down the steps, and danced, with all their friends to Paradise Park to celebrate the very first celebration of Love Others Day! And it was an amazingly great day!!

The End...

Or is it the,

Another Step?

ABOUT THE AUTHOR

Eileen DiStasio-Clark is the second oldest of four children. She is the mother of eleven children and grandmother to twenty-three grandchildren, to date. As a member of The Church of Jesus Christ of Latter-Day Saints, she serves in various positions, teaching, leading, and ministering to children, youth, and adults. Currently, she is also a Family History Missionary. Eileen established the Pursuit of Excellence Institute of Family Education, a non-profit organization focused on strengthening the family. Presently she holds an A.A., a B.A., and an M.A. in Clinical Psychology and is working on the completion of her Doctoral Degree.

9 798330 556397